Smitten

&

Bitten

Eila Algood

ISBN: 9798412275215

Cover photograph by: Eila Algood
Cover design by: Art Painter
Library of Congress Control Number: 2018675309
Printed in the United States of America

Dedication

To every person who ever felt marginalized
or unaccepted or different.
The world needs us each to honor our
uniqueness and live our truth.

Table of Contents

Chapter 1

Trial on the Trail

The rattlesnake leapt at her bare, tanned leg, sinking its fangs into the soft, delicate skin. Cherise screamed. The snake released her and took off into the brush. Her leg began to swell as she collapsed onto the dirt. She'd brought nothing with her, not even her cell phone. Afraid for her life, she forced her body up so she could walk back down the trail. After ten slow steps, with her body reacting to the venom, she was forced to sit on the damp dirt.

Cherise had been running up Tongue Mountain in the Adirondack mountains of New York, overlooking picturesque, Lake George when she spotted the snake. She stopped short, not sure what to do next. Without training in how to handle such a situation, she was terrified and froze in place. There were lots of dangers around her home in Manhattan, but nothing prepared her for this. The sound of the rattle put her into a panic attack. Her ability to think clearly was gone so instead of staying put, she turned and that's when it struck.

She called for help, yelling loudly. This wasn't a well-travelled path, but it was a summer weekend, and she was hoping she'd get lucky. Within five minutes a group of teenagers, six local kids, heard her cry for help. They'd grown up in these mountains and knew she needed immediate medical attention.

"I'm Martin and we're going to help you," the oldest boy said.
Cherise looked at him with tears in her eyes and began to mumble.

"Chris and Beth, you take her feet. Pat and Bernie, thighs and back, me and Wanda will hold her upper body. Be sure to keep the snakebite area lower than her heart. On three." Martin said.

"Who died and made you boss?" Bernie said.

"Really, Bernie, chill out. This woman is in distress." Chris replied.
Bernie rolled his eyes but stepped in with everyone to help. There was no time to

waste, she needed to get to a doctor immediately and it would take them ten minutes to get her back down the trail. When they arrived in the parking lot, Chris called out,

"Help, please help! Someone with a car, this woman needs to get to the hospital!" It was a small gravel parking lot surrounded by tall, scented pine trees. The smell comforted Cherise as she was placed in some stranger's back seat.

"I'm gonna go with her, you guys go ahead. I'll catch up later." Martin said.

"I'll go too." Said Beth who had a bit of a crush on Martin.

"Not necessary."
Beth got in the car next to Cherise; Martin sat in front alongside the tall, dark, stranger with a kind face.

"I'm Martin, thanks for doing this." As he put out his hand to shake hers.

"Georgia Clay; where are we going?" The stranger asked.

"There's a clinic in town, can you get us there?" Martin asked.

Georgia was a tall, dark-skinned African American woman with short, black hair and dark glossy eyes. She had a hint of a southern accent. There was something strong yet gentle in her manner. Martin was much the opposite. Short for his age of 15, with blonde hair, grey-blue eyes, and fair skin. He was mature for his age and knew how to hold himself among adults.

Meanwhile in the back, was Cherise, medium height and build, spiky brown hair with bleached streaks, light complexion, moaning in pain.   Beth who was tall for 15, almost six feet with wavy red long hair tied back for the hike, tried to comfort Cherise by asking her questions about Bolton. Her face was filled with more freckles than clear skin and she had a quirky sense of humor.

"What's your favorite island on the lake?" Beth asked Cherise.

"Uh, what? Um, Picnic Island. Ow, this hurts." Whined Cherise.

"You're going to be okay. Everything's going to be okay" Beth said.
Beth didn't believe what she was saying but she'd heard it enough on television shows that she figured it would work. Her voice was gentle and soothing, which provided Cherise a meditative experience.

Georgia pulled up to the emergency entrance of the small first aid station downtown, just next to the post office and grocery store. Although Bolton Landing was a tiny town, the summer population was large enough to warrant a small medical facility.

"Wait here, I'll get help" Martin said as he flew out of the car and into the clinic.
Two people came out with a stretcher and helped Cherise up, whisking her away inside.

"Martin, why don't you and your friend go back to the trail, and I'll stay here and get things sorted out with, what's her name?" Georgia said.

"Yea, I will, once she's been admitted." Martin said.
They all went in and gave what little information they had about Cherise to the receptionist.

"Thanks for bringing her in so quickly. She'll be okay now. No need to wait." The nurse came out to tell them.

They went outside the small clinic and Georgia offered to drive them back to the trailhead.

It was two hours later when Cherise was released from the clinic; her leg bandaged up where the rattlesnake bit her. Her eyes filled with tears as her sixty-year-old mom walked through the tattered doorway.

"Cherise, sweetheart, are you okay?" Her mother asked.

"It was a nightmare, Mom. I don't even remember how I got here. A damn snake bit my leg so quickly and then I was on the ground, yelling for help."

"I brought your cell phone. Here you go. Why didn't you take it?"

"Really, Mom?   That doesn't help. There's next to no cell service here anyway."

"That's   true."   Chimed   in   the receptionist.   "There's   no   reception   on Tongue Mountain anyway. It's a good thing those kids came by when then did and were able to have that lady drive you here."

Cherise remembered none of it. The receptionist wrote the names of the people who brought her in on a piece of paper. Cherise wanted to find them to offer her gratitude.   Once   at   her   mom's   lakeside cottage, Cherise looked up the phone numbers of the people who were so kind in getting her to the clinic. Martin Williams and Beth McFarlane were easy to find in the phone book. She called each of their homes;

spoke with their mother's and then them to offer her gratitude. She invited to have them over for dinner later in the week.

"Do you have a phone number for Georgia?" Cherise asked Martin.

"I never met her until that day, so no. I think she said she lives in Connecticut."
Cherise did a search on the Internet and located a phone number for Georgia Clay in New Haven, Connecticut. She called and left a message.

Chapter 2

Connecticut

Connection

It was a week later when Cherise's phone rang with phone number having a 203 area code.

"Hello, is this Miss Cherise?"

"Yes, who's calling please?" she replied cautiously.

"Georgia. Georgia Clay. Remember me?"

"Oh, I'm so glad you called. Thank you so much for getting me to the clinic. They said I could have died if you and the kids had not acted so quickly.

"You are very welcome. It was the only kind thing to do. You poor thing how's your leg?"

"Feeling much better. I'll be heading home later in the week. I would very much like to show my gratitude. When can I come out to New Haven and buy you lunch?"

"Oh, Miss Cherise there is no need for you to do that."

"It would mean a lot to me to thank you in person. There's a 10am out of Penn Station that gets into New Haven at 11:30 on Saturday. You pick a nice restaurant and I'll meet you there." Cherise said.

"Alright, I'm free on Saturday, but I insist on meeting you at the train station. I'll be there at 11:30 sharp."

"Fabulous. See you then."

After a few days, Cherise felt well enough to go home to her place in NYC and back to work where she was consumed catching up after her two-week vacation to Lake George. There wasn't a moment to think of anything else. She barely got on the train to New Haven before the doors shut. Cherise did not remember seeing Georgia at all during her snake bite ordeal, so she had no idea who she'd be looking for as she exited the train onto the hot, humid platform. She walked outside the station, hopeful that Georgia would recognize her. A moment later,

"Well, well, you are looking much better than the last time I saw you." Georgia said as she reached out to greet Cherise.

Cherise was amazed at Georgia's tall, statuesque appearance and mesmerized by her glossy black eyes.

"Uh, oh, yes, yes. She laughed It's great to meet you, officially."

Georgia's southern hospitality came through as she put her arm around Cherise, guiding her to the car.

"What kind of food do you like?" Georgia asked.

"This is for you, not me. Let's go to a favorite place of yours." Cherise insisted.

"Okay, you asked for it." Georgia laughed.

Georgia had a deep, hearty laugh. Cherise felt drawn in by Georgia's voice and gentle hospitality.

"I'm so grateful to you" Cherise began to say.

"Miss Cherise, you have expressed your gratitude many times. Tell me about yourself. Where are you from? What do you do in New York City? How did you come to be on that trail?"

"My family spent many summers in Bolton Landing.   My mom inherited a summer cottage there from my beloved grandmother. I had an argument with my mom that morning and flew out of the house to the trail. My mind was not focused in the moment, which is why I didn't spot that snake. What brought you to the trail?"

"I gave a workshop at Silver Bay. That's a beautiful place."

"What was the topic?"

"Integrating Spirituality into the Workplace." Georgia said

"How do you do that?"

"Very carefully. Georgia said with a chuckle. What do you do in New York City?"

"Too much, really. I work in the financial district and play in SoHo."

"Tell me about playing in SoHo." Georgia requested.

"I minored in art and have been showing some of my three-dimensional art pieces at a SoHo gallery owned by my friend Carlota. I would really like to hear about your workshop."

"Having been raised by a Catholic mother and Baptist father who loved their religions, provided me an assortment of information as a child. Because they could not agree as to which religion I should attend, they exposed me to both and allowed me to choose for myself. That freedom encouraged me to learn the basics of many religions. Once I knew the rules and responsibilities, I searched deeper into the spirituality, realizing we are all spiritual beings."

"I'm not sure I agree with that." Cherise said.

"What?"

"That we are all spiritual beings. I see a lot of greed and power-hungry people in the financial world, and they are not so spiritual." Cherise said.

"At the core, without the money, without the power, without the ego, we are inherently spiritual. That's what I bring to the university setting. There are many intelligent people in that world and sometimes they follow their ego more than their intuition. My intention is to connect people to the spirit of who they are, without the titles and accolades." Georgia said.

"I know many people who could benefit from your workshop. Not just those in the university setting, including me."

"You don't come across egotistical or power hungry." Georgia stated.

"I could agree with that, but I often grapple with the infamous questions of life. Who am I and why am I here?"

"What is the answer?"

"If I knew, it wouldn't be a question." Cherise smiled.

"I believe we each know the answer to those questions deep down inside of our being. The challenge is knowing how to hear the answers."

"How do you hear the answers?"

"By taking time and space to connect with my spirit. Which can be through meditation, or simply being in nature." Georgia stated.

"That's why I love being in Bolton Landing. When I walk through the big pines and see how the sun is filtered through their branches while breathing in the sweet pine scent, I become present. It's inspiring." Cherise closes her eyes and takes a deep breath.   When she opened her eyes and looked at Georgia, she recited a poem she had written while walking through the woods near Lake George.

"Golden glow all around.

Touches of orange, red and brown.

Am I as beautiful as what I see?

Is it the same god that created me?

Bare branches are arms outstretched to greet me.

Branches on high spread their wings to shield me.

The rhythm of nature surrounds and engulfs me in its beauty."

Georgia was quiet as she listened and felt Cherise's words flow through her, moved by the essence of the poetry, and mesmerized by her gaze.

"I wrote that, or should I say, it came to me while walking through the woods during autumn near Lake George."

"Exactly. That's when we can hear the answers." Georgia said slowly.

Needing to break the seriousness of the moment, Cherise replied

"Unless a snake bites your leg!"

They both laughed.

The conversation continued as they ate at a small Indian restaurant, barely taking a breath in between bites and words. After leaving the restaurant, they walked to downtown New Haven.

"That was delicious and enjoyable. Thank you, Cherise."

"My pleasure. It's been wonderful getting to know you, but I don't want to keep you all day. I realize you must have things to do other than talk to me."

"I do need to stop by the Yale School of Architecture Gallery. Care to join me? You can walk around while I pick up some drawings."

"Sounds fun. Are you sure?"

"Miss Cherise, I never say anything I don't mean. If you've never been there, you may find it interesting."

"I've never been there. Georgia, Miss feels a bit formal. Would you mind simply calling me Cherise?"
Georgia laughed that deep, gruff laugh as she nodded yes.

"Putting Miss in front of a woman's name was commonplace where I grew up. It's not so much formality but respect. But I will honor your request."

"This place is amazing. Cherise said as they walked into the architecture gallery. I like the projects being worked on."

"I'll be back in a few minutes. Wait here" Georgia said.

"No problem."

They wandered into a few art galleries, stopping for a tea break as they talked their way through New Haven until it was nearly six o'clock.

"Looks like it's time to eat again. How about we go back to my house where I can fix us something to eat? I'd like to drop off this tube of drawings." Georgia said.

Cherise found her time with Georgia more enjoyable than with anyone she'd ever known so it was easy for her to say yes.

The house was a beautiful purple and tan Victorian with a wraparound porch. When they entered, a feeling of familiarity overwhelmed Cherise. Something felt so comfortable with Georgia and now her home. Spicy smells filled the air as a big calico kitty rubbed up against her leg.

"That's Rainbow, my girlfriend." Georgia said as she played Etta James on her sound system.

"Hi Rainbow, it's my pleasure to meet you." Cherise said as she reached down to pet her long, soft, colorful fur.

"The kitchen's back here."

"I want to help.   Put me to work." Cherise said.

"Be careful what you ask for." Georgia said as she laughed.

The two prepared a simple but tasty meal of rice and sautéed vegetables in a spicy sauce.

"Wine for you?"

"Lovely, I'll pour." Cherise said.

They continued they're chatting while eating and sharing in a glass of chardonnay. Cherise inadvertently stared at Georgia.

"Do I have lettuce on my face or something?" Georgia said jokingly.

"Oh, uh, no. I'm sorry. I didn't mean to stare. Your skin, it's so smooth and your eyes. I've never..."

"Never seen a black woman before?" Georgia said with a grin.

"Oh god, nothing like that. I just, I'm..." Cherise stammered.

Just then, the front door slammed shut and a tall, dark-skinned man entered the kitchen.

With an accent he said hello and introduced himself to Cherise.

"You must be the snake bitten woman I've heard about." He said.

Cherise felt embarrassed. She was just about to tell Georgia that she felt a strong attraction to her, and now this African man walked in.

"Yes, that's me. I'm Cherise, nice to meet you." She said calmly, hiding her surprise.

"I'm Kwesi. I've heard a lot about you from Georgia. So glad you're A-Okay" he said with a smile.

"I didn't expect to see you until later, but you're welcome to join us." Georgia said.

"I had dinner out and have some work to do. It's nice to meet you, Cherise. I'll see you later, Georgia. I'll be in my office."

Kwesi left the dining area and went upstairs.

"Sorry for the interruption, but I didn't think he'd be home tonight."

"Home? I didn't realize you lived with someone." Cherise said.

"I met him on a tennis court about ten years ago. He liked the way I swung a racket, and I liked his sense of humor. Now what were we saying before he came in?

"It's not important.   I should be heading home soon." Cherise said, feeling awkward.

"Oh, I haven't offered you dessert yet. I have some fresh berries and whipped cream."

"Thanks, but I don't want to ride the train too late. How about I help you with the dishes and then go?"

"You are welcomed to stay over. We have a guest room you could use. Then we wouldn't have to hurry." Georgia said kindly.

Cherise loved how she felt with Georgia and was torn between getting the hell out of there now that she knew Georgia had a man in her life or staying just to spend more time with Georgia.

"Can I use your bathroom?"

"Of course, down the hall, on the right."

Cherise went into the bathroom, locked the door, stared into the mirror and whispered "What should I do? I have never felt this way about another human being, yet it must be wrong. She's involved with someone. Where does that leave me? And he's a man, not a woman. She might be homophobic for all I know. I want to run out, yet my heart says stay. Grandma, help me here. Give me a sign to stay or go. I really need some help." With that, she flushed the toilet as if she used it and went back down the hall. By the time she reached the table, and opened her mouth to state that she'd leave, there was a huge clap of thunder. She looked up to the ceiling as if to acknowledge the message from her grandmother.

"Perhaps I'll stay. Traveling by train in the rain at night is a fright." Cherise said.

"You are quite poetic. Okay then. Let's go whip some cream!" Georgia said with a big smile.

Cherise reflected on the day she spent with Georgia as she lay in the large, soft, fluffy bed, gazing at the streetlight through the tall, old-style double hung window in the distance. She felt a strange but welcome comfort with Georgia. The bedroom had a sweet, familiar scent, which reminded her of her grandmother. It was only moments until she drifted off into a peaceful sleep.

Chapter 3

Just a Job

"Cherise, come into my office in ten minutes." Cynthia said assertively as she poked her head in the doorway.

Cherise was staring out the window at the gray sky over Manhattan, seeing nothing, hearing nothing; her mind drifting into an alternate reality.

"Cherise! Her boss called louder as she knocked on the door. Ten minutes."

Cherise spun her chair around, having been snapped out of the trance like state and replied, "I will be there. Shall I bring anything?"

"Nothing."

Cherise wondered what her boss was up to. She was keeping up with her work okay, although she'd been a little less focused since the snakebite or was it since she'd met Georgia? Ah, Georgia with those deep brown eyes and her strong melodic voice. Maybe that was the root of her zoning out.

"Come in and close the door behind you." Cynthia said coldly.

The office was a large a corner location with tall windows facing the East River. On a clear day, the sunrise would be visible, but today a Nor'easter was on its way and clouds covered most of the region. The glass top desk was clean, neat, and void of papers, much different than Cherise's.   Cynthia motioned for Cherise to sit in one of the two light wood chairs with deep purple cushions placed squarely facing the desk. After a few moments of small talk, Cynthia said,

"I called you in because your performance has been off the mark. I know you had that snake incident and perhaps it's related to that. I'm getting pressure from the higher ups to inspire you to be more productive. Your stock sales are low this month."

Cherise felt nauseous with a horrible sensation in the pit of her stomach. She hadn't expected this; didn't see it coming and was unprepared to answer as Cynthia pressured her for a response.

"I have been working seventy hours a week and have a few deals in process. What exactly are you speaking of? I could respond better if I knew the particulars."

"Staring out the window is not working. Your numbers are down. It's Monday, and it's imperative we see some results by next Thursday."

Cherise walked out, grabbed her jacket from her own office and left the building. She walked twenty blocks to the little gallery in SoHo that was showing her 3D artwork. Her face was wet with cold tears as she stepped into the warm, art filled space. She took her first deep breath upon entering. The fifteen-foot-high walls were whitewashed brick with colorful three-dimensional art pieces hanging high and low. The floor was chestnut brown wood with a matte finish. The gloominess of the day did not enter this brightly lit space.

"Risy, what a surprise! Oh my, you look sad, come in and have some tea." Gary said as he put his arm around Cherise, offering some compassion. Cherise met Gary three years ago at a party and they became close friends. It was he who encouraged her artist abilities.

"I'd rather not go into the story; suffice to say I had some bad news at work."

"I shan't ask any details then. Would you like to see how I've displayed your work? Follow me." He said with a big smile as they walked through the gallery.

It was a great distraction from the issues at work to be in the bright, warm, and friendly space for a few minutes. Seeing her artwork displayed in this gallery was surreal. She loved doing art as a kid, but her parents insisted she choose a profession in economics to support herself. Her father, who was a corrections officer, used to tell her "No child of mine will waste time studying art." Cherise dabbled in it during her spare time, which she had very little of since becoming a stockbroker on Wall St.

When she arrived back at work, she had a renewed sense of determination. She worked tirelessly for the next week and a half. On the next Thursday at three o'clock, she went into the meeting with Cynthia and the other bosses.

"Cherise, you've been one of our top producers. I called you in on Monday, requesting that you improve your performance." Cynthia said.
At this point Cherise had a hard time focusing. Were they going to fire her, she wondered? She knew she'd been a bit off, but if they fired her, well then screw them. She had some savings to live off and then she

could spend her days doing the art she felt most passionate about.

"Did you hear me, Cherise?" Cynthia asked.

"No, I did not. Can you repeat what you said?"

"You exceeded our expectations in your performance, and we will be giving you a bonus. Your stock sales are up twenty percent. Excellent job!"

With a cordial smile, she thanked them. Yet inside herself, she was underwhelmed. The incident had her reflecting on her choice to work in the financial district when art was her true passion. She was in an introspective space when she arrived back in her office, closing the door behind her. The cell phone rang. Without looking at who was calling, she answered.

"Hello." Cherise answered glumly.

"Well, hello Cherise, this is"

"Georgia. Georgia Clay. How are you?" Cherise said cheerfully.

"Do you have a moment?" Georgia asked.

"Your timing is impeccable. Absolutely." Cherise said as she sat in her chocolate-colored leather desk chair. For the first time in a while, she felt extremely present as she listened to Georgia speak.

"I had such a lovely time with you in New Haven last month and I have reason to come to New York City on Saturday. I was wondering if you would like to get together again."

Cherise felt transported to another dimension as she heard Georgia's voice, remembering her brown eyes; touching the leather armrest and wondering what it would be like to touch Georgia's dark skin.

"Yes, I'd love to get together. I have one commitment on Saturday that you could be part of if you want."

"I don't want to infringe on your plans." Georgia said.

"It's nothing like that. My friend will be the séance conductor at a psychic development school in midtown. It's from 7-9 and if you're up for it, we could go together."

"I'm quite the skeptic, but I'm willing to try."

"I'll email you my address and directions this afternoon. My boss is on her way, so it's best I go now.

"I look forward to seeing you then." Georgia said.

As Cherise pressed the end button on her phone, she sat back in her chair, sporting the biggest smile she'd had in weeks.

As soon as Cherise arrived home, she kicked off her shoes, poured herself some tea and sat down at her laptop to write to Georgia. "Dear Georgia, I was thrilled" then she'd back space thinking her word choice was too emotional. "I was happy to hear from you today. It had been a horrific week" then back space and delete to "It's been a challenging week at work. I'm looking forward to getting together on Saturday. Rather than meeting at my apartment, would you like to meet at Lindy's for a slice of cheesecake? It's across from Penn Station. Let's say, 2 o'clock. How to sign her name became a fifteen-minute decision. She wanted to write "Excitedly yours, Cherise"; could not bear to write "Regards, Cherise". After looking up synonyms in the thesaurus for five minutes, she settled for "See you Saturday, Cherise".

Chapter 4

Magic in Manhattan

Saturdays were usually a reason to sleep late, but there was too much excitement in the air for sleep. Cherise jumped out of bed at seven and began her preparations for Georgia's visit. She wasn't sure they'd come back to her apartment, but at least it would be neat and clean if they did. She took out her favorite display of five red candles but decided that red was a bit too bold, so out she went to get something more appropriate. After two hours of shopping, Cherise returned with two white and three black candles to be placed on her birch coffee table. On the kitchen table she arranged two calla lilies in a crystal vase that belonged to her grandma. The place sparkled; it was so clean, and she prepared a stick of incense which she'd light when and if Georgia came back with her. At one o'clock, she took a quick shower, put on her black jeans; white V-neck tee shirt, short black leather jacket and headed out the door.

It was a cool, sunny autumn day in New York. The streets were buzzing with cars, sirens were blaring, kids were yelling, horns were honking, but Cherise heard none of it. She was walking briskly to meet the woman that mysteriously appeared at the Tongue Mountain trail just in the nick of time. The woman with the deep dark eyes, chocolate brown complexion and melodic voice with a hint of southern drawl. Cherise arrived at Lindy's by 1:45, just to be sure she didn't miss Georgia's arrival, but she was too antsy to sit, so she walked up and down the street until 2. At 2:05, her phone vibrated, and she read the text: "The train was delayed, on my way." "I'm at Lindy's. See you soon." She replied.

Cherise felt foolish for making such a fuss over this meeting. After all, she thought, I hardly know this woman. Sure, she was kind to me, but I think I've been fantasizing that I have feelings for her. I need to wake up and realize that she's simply a new friend. Nothing more." With that, she took a sip of her tea and closed her eyes for a moment. By the time she opened her eyes, Georgia was stepping through the door of the restaurant and walked towards her. Cherise's heart began beating fast and she could not help but smile. They shared a cordial embrace and sat down at the booth. Georgia looked radiant.

"You're looking happy today, Cherise."

"In this moment, I am. How was your trip here today?" Cherise replied.

"Aside from the delay, it was uneventful."
With that they ordered.

"Can I have a slice of mocha cheesecake with blueberries on the side and a coffee please?" Georgia asked.

"I'll take a refill on my tea and a slice of plain cheesecake." Cherise said

"Milk in the coffee, ma'am?" The waiter asked.

"Yes, thank you."

"What have you been up to?" Cherise asked.

"My classes are going very well this semester. I love teaching when the students are engaged and interested, which most are this term."

"What exactly do you teach?"

"Introduction to architecture for undergraduate students considering a career in architecture."

"My uncle was an architect and I remember looking at some of his drawings when I was a teenager. . I thought they were awesome, but complicated."

"With the advent of computer assisted design, it's gotten easier and much more efficient. I spent a few years with an architecture firm, doing design for renovation as well as new construction.”

“Where?”

“San Francisco.”

“How did you change to teaching?”

“I’ve always wanted to teach, since I was in high school. I knew I needed practical experience to be an effective teacher, so the job was a means to an end.”

The waiter returned.

“Mocha for you and plain for you. Here’s your coffee and cream. I’ll be right back with more hot water.”

“Thank you.” Georgia said, “This looks scrumptious. Would you like a taste?”
Cherise took a forkful and closed her eyes as she placed it in her mouth.

"Mmmm, this is delightful, she said. Here, have a bite of mine too. It's not as exotic, but"

"Plain is pure, I'll have a taste." Georgia said.

The two continued to enjoy their dessert and conversation as the restaurant became filled with people. Once done, Cherise insisted on paying the bill and out the door they went, into the cool, afternoon city air.

"I live about a thirty-minute walk from here. Are you up for it?" Cherise asked.

"I wore my walking shoes, in anticipation of wandering through the city."

"I thought we could pick up something for dinner along the way. The séance is at 7, we need to leave by 6:30, so an early dinner is best."

"That's good for me."

After making a few stops in clothing stores, they went to a corner grocery. As is common in New York, the shelves were packed with items and the aisles were very narrow. Space is at a premium and every inch was well utilized. The store smelled delicious with the aroma of freshly baked breads and homemade soup in the air.

"How about a sprouted grain bread with their soup and some salad?" Cherise asked.

"I could do without the salad as I had some for lunch. I could sauté some of this fresh spinach.

"Sounds delicious."
Cherise's apartment was on the top floor in a four-story walk-up building, in the Chelsea area of Manhattan. The exterior was red brick with tall, double hung windows and a

tall stoop with wrought iron railings leading up to the eight-foot-tall front wooden door.

"This is a charming building. I love the old-style architecture." Georgia said.

"You'll love the inside then. It's been restored and filled with character".

There was a small foyer with an oak floor and oak railed wooden staircase. As they ascended, Georgia was looking at every detail along the way, commenting on the quality of craftsmanship. Once to the top, she said,

"This seems to be a great way to stay in shape!"
Cherise opened the door and motioned for Georgia to go in first.

"I love your wood floors and the natural light is exquisite."

"Let's bring the groceries into the kitchen and I'll show you around." Cherise said.

The kitchen was small and functional in the middle of the apartment. They walked down the short hallway to the living room, in the front of the building, which although it faced north, the six-foot tall, double hung windows offered a generous amount of light. The furnishings were simple and streamlined. There was a handcrafted wooden rocker by the window, which seemed to be the focal point of the room. Light, sheer curtains framed the windows and popped with the green; clay plastered walls. The ten-foot ceiling created an expansive feeling in a space that was about twelve feet wide by sixteen feet long. A contemporary wool rug with large green leaf patterns edged in gold grounded the space. A large maple wall unit sat opposite the windows. The cherry secretary brought a bit of old-style charm with the modern laptop sitting on top.

"What a charming place you have." Cherise put on a playlist of her favorite jazz, starting with Ella Fitzgerald.

"Thanks. How about something to drink?"

"Some bubbly water would be great. My Funny Valentine was one of my mom's favorite songs." Cherise went to pour their drinks and a moment later, Georgia came into the kitchen.

"Here you go." Cherise said as she handed the glass of water to Georgia.

"To our health and friendship." Georgia said as they clinked glasses.

"Would you like to see my studio?"

Georgia motioned for Cherise to lead the way. As they entered the room, which faced south, the afternoon sun was streaming in through the two tall windows. In the middle of the room was a large worktable scattered with partially done projects. Shelves with supplies lined a wall. Track lighting scrolled along the ceiling.

"I feel inspired to create just being in here." Georgia said.
Cherise smiled and looked into Georgia's eyes as she said,

"I have something for you. This is a piece I made when I was convalescing after the snake bite."

"Oh, Cherise, this is special. I like the combination of red and gold as a backdrop for the white snake, which is made from, is that rope?"

"It is twine wrapped around a piece of wire, soaked in a white gloss poly finish."

They talked about art and the creative process as they made their way back to the kitchen to prepare dinner. The kitchen was small, and their arms touched as they prepared their food. Cherise felt excited by their physical touch and wondered what Georgia was feeling. They sat at the small round glass table and began to eat.

"Are you smitten with me, Cherise?" Dramatically, Cherise put her head down on her arm which was laying on the table, and for the first time that day found herself at a loss for words.

"Don't worry. I saw it when we met at the station. There's chemistry here. And although I have only dated people of my race, well, I'm open to this. It feels like we were destined to meet, and I don't interfere with destiny."

Cherise lifted her head and placed her hand on Georgia's soft, warm arm, whispering,

"Can I kiss you?"

The two leaned in and softly kissed. Cherise stood up to get closer to Georgia, to kiss her. She moved in, touching her face, and kissed her more passionately this time. Caressing her soft skin, gazing into her eyes, she smiled. There was chemistry all right. Cherise hadn't felt such tingling or racing heart since the snakebite!

"I can't believe I'm going to say this, but I'm glad that snake bit me."

"I'm glad you said it first!" Georgia said with a laugh.

The air was emotionally charged. Georgia stopped Cherise from removing her shirt.

"I think it'd be better to finish dinner now." Georgia said.

"Yes, yes, you are correct." Cherise said as she buttoned up Georgia's shirt
The two completed dinner and began to walk to the Séance center. It was a cool autumn evening, so they kept a brisk pace. The sky was clear, and the city was a buzz with people and traffic. It was near sunset as they arrived at their destination.

"This looks like an office building." Georgia said surprised

"What were you expecting? Red lights and a crystal ball outside?" Cherise joked.
They entered the historic five-story building and stepped into the small elevator. When they got off on the fifth floor, there were ten people standing outside an office door.

"We must be very early." Georgia said.

"Just ten minutes to seven. Francesca has never late, but often arrived just in time to begin."

They stood, waiting, and talking, finding it difficult to not touch one another. Although Manhattan tends to be gay friendly, one never knows who may be homophobic, so they thought it best to play it safe.

"It's after seven. Maybe something came up for her." Georgia suggested.

Cherise checked her phone and saw a text from Francesca: *My daughter had an accident, and I am at the ER with her. Can you conduct the séance tonight? The key for the office is in the lock box #4825. Or you can just cancel.*

"She had to go to the ER with her daughter and asked me to conduct the séance."

"Have you done that before?" Georgia asked.

"Many times." Cherise said and then she addressed the people waiting outside the office door.

"Good evening, everyone. My name is Cherise, and I will be conducting tonight as Francesca had a family emergency. Please follow me in, take a seat and we will begin shortly."

Cherise motioned for Georgia to sit next to her in the circle of fifteen chairs as she set up for the event.

"Hello again. I apologize for the late start. Can you all stay for an hour and a half from now?"

The people nodded yes.

"I've been conducting séances here for three years. I was a student and now teach level one psychic development. You are in good hands tonight. For this evening, I will ask each person to say his or her name. I'll turn on music and turn out the lights. Is everyone okay with sitting in the dark?"

"I get claustrophobic sometimes" a fair-haired middle-aged man said.

"If you want to be in the circle, I suggest you focus on the space in the room. If you feel too uneasy about sitting in the dark, then it is best for you to leave now."

"I think I'll be okay." He said.

"We'll go around again and say our names once in the dark. I'll do a prayer for protection followed by a guided meditation for twenty minutes and then we will open for spirit communication. Any questions or concerns?" Cherise asked.

"What if something scary happens." A young woman asked.

"It is very important to focus on what you want to experience tonight and to keep your focus positive. It's scarier on the street than it is in here." Cherise joked.

For the next half an hour, they meditated and sat quietly.

"Please speak up if you have any physical sensations or odd thoughts pop into your head as they can be a message from Spirit." Cherise encouraged.

There were a few messages shared back and forth. Cherise whispered to Georgia,

"How are you doing?"

"Okay. I'm okay."

Then, a certified medium that was attending the séance began to speak.

"This is Richard, can I come to you, Georgia?" He asked.

"Yes, Richard." She replied.

"I have an image of an older woman, perhaps your mother. She shows me a pink cape and says you'd understand."

"Oh my, yes. I had a pink cape when I was a child. She made it for me. I begged her. How did you know about that?" Georgia asked.

"She wants you to know that it is really her. She mentions an argument between you and her. She says that it's okay; you can let it go now. She is at peace and only wants for your happiness. Did you have an argument with her just before she died?" Richard asked.

Georgia begins to cry. "Yes, I yelled at her over something ridiculous and she died the next week. I felt awful."

"She is smiling and asks for you to let it go. She asks that you remember all the loving times you shared together, especially the summer you spent in the islands. I'm getting Grand Cayman." He said.

"I spent my sixteenth birthday there with my mom and her family. That's amazing." Georgia said.

"Your mother is bringing forth a young man. It's her grandson and he is about nine years old. She wants you to know he is with her and doing well. That's all for now." Richard said.

Georgia began to sob. She could not believe her ears. Her baby, who died as an infant, was with her mother. She thought about him every day and wondered if he was okay. She could not stop the tears and quickly got up and found her way to the door.

"Georgia, are you there." Cherise asked.

"I believe she just left. I can hear the elevator door closing." Richard said.

Cherise was leading this circle and could not get up and follow Georgia. She stayed with the group for another hour until it was time to close. After the last person left, Cherise locked up and headed outside. She looked around for Georgia, but the street was quiet. She checked her phone. There was nothing. No voicemail. No text. Without hesitation, she dialed Georgia, but it went right to voicemail.

"Georgia, it's Cherise. What happened? Are you okay? Please call me, I'm concerned about you."

There was no response that night, the next day, and the entire week. Cherise was upset. She had a deep need to communicate with Georgia, but her calls went unreturned. After an entire week without contact, Cherise arrived home and felt very angry.

"What could be so terrible, that she can't talk to me? Can't answer my calls? This feels very dramatic. Maybe she's not right for me.   I don't want to be in relationship with a drama queen anyway." Cherise yelled as she paced around her apartment.

Rather than get deeper into the anger, she decided to go out. In fact, she thought it best to go back to a séance where she knew she'd get some understanding and compassion. Communing with Spirit had a way of relaxing her. She was the first one in the door at the Séance Center.

"Hey, Cherise, thanks for covering for me last week. You're a lifesaver!" Francesca said.

"I need some emotional lifesaving myself tonight. How's your daughter?"

"She's doing well. It was just a sprain, nothing broken, thank goodness. How can I help you tonight?" Francesca asked.

"Play some peaceful music for the meditation. That will help. Just being here is helping me relax." Cherise said.

"Sit up here, on my left. We'll have a great evening."

Francesca's voice was calming to Cherise. She could feel herself drifting into a deep place during the guided meditation.

"Bring yourself back up and out of meditation, becoming aware of your surroundings. Move your hands and arms as you become more fully in your body." Francesca said to the séance participants as she turned off the music.

Cherise felt tranquil and her mind was quiet for the first time in a week. She enjoyed the energy of the séance. It provided a familiar comfort, like one of her mother's handmade blankets. After a few moments, someone spoke up.

"I have a message, but I am not sure who it is for." Gloria said.

"Begin sharing the message and perhaps the person who can best relate will emerge." Francesca said.

"This woman is very upset. She wants to get a message to someone to say she is sorry, for upsetting him or her. It's a woman who isn't here. Cherise, I think this is for you." Gloria said.

"Can you repeat what you said, I wasn't listening."

"There is a woman here with a little boy who says she is sorry for upsetting someone. I am asking her for a name. George? Do you know someone named George?"

"Georgia, yes, I know a Georgia." Cherise perked up.

"Okay, then, tell Georgia her mother is sorry for upsetting her. Tell her the little boy whose name is Andy or Randy, is well and sits on the red-checkered window seat in her house each night in her living room. He's with her a lot. He does not blame her. He loves her. That's all for now." Gloria said.

"Thank you, Gloria. I will try to relay the message."

"I have one more thing. Tell this to Georgia in person.
With that, Francesca closed the circle. Cherise left as soon as the lights went on. She felt excited, wanting to get out and walk in the cool night air. Against all logic, she

texted Georgia: "I got a message at séance tonight from your mother that she asked me to deliver to you in person." With that, Cherise went home to pack for her tropical vacation.

Chapter 5

Hawai'i Happenstance

It had been a chilly autumn day when Cherise booked a two-week trip to Hawai'i. She began her vacation on Waikiki beach, but the crowds reminded her too much of Manhattan. She took a flight to the big island of Hawaii. She'd taken a unique approach and went where her heart told her to go. The first stop was the rainforest area north of Hilo. She enjoyed walking the path to see towering Akaka Falls. As she stood, gazing up at the falls, a tall, dark-skinned woman walked up next to her. For a split second, she thought it was Georgia, but that was quickly proven incorrect.

"Are you okay?" The woman asked.

"Oh, I'm sorry, you look so much like a friend of mine." Cherise responded.

"You look so shocked, I thought something was wrong." The woman replied.

"No, everything's fine. Thanks for asking." Cherise said with a forced smile.

As Cherise walked away, looking at the bright red flowers hanging from trees she wondered if she really was fine. She wondered why she still even thought of Georgia when it had been weeks since Georgia left without a word. This trip was to clear her mind, relax her body and sooth her spirit.   She'd spend no more moments thinking about someone who clearly had some serious mental issues.

By day ten, Cherise found her way to the northern tip of the island in a place known as Kohala. As she drove along the coast highway on the western side of the island where it was hot, dry, and desert like, she saw a brilliant rainbow arcing over the road. It was afternoon and there was a light rain off in the distance. The landscape began to change to green as she rounded the northern tip of the island. She saw the sign "Hawi Town" and drove slowly, looking for the road to turn down for her bed and breakfast.   She arrived at five and was greeted by a friendly woman in overalls.

"Aloha. You must be Cherise." She said as she reached out to hug her.

"Hi, yes." Cherise said.

As they had a momentary embrace, Cherise feeling awkward, the woman invited her to follow her to her room for the night.

"Your place is amazing. What's the mountain across the ocean there?" Cherise asked as she pointed northwest.

"That's Haleakala on the island of Maui."

"Wow, it's so tall and majestic." Cherise said.

"Hawaii is filled with magic too."

"Is it possible to hike down and swim in the ocean here?" Cherise asked.

"No one swims out there as it is one of the most treacherous channels in the Pacific. If you want to jump in and cool off, Mahukona is a quick ten-minute drive."

"How long have you lived here?" Cherise inquired.

"About ten years now, originally from New York."

"No kidding? Small world. That's where I live."

After bringing her bag into her room she thought a swim was just what she needed and headed off before sunset. It was a local swim spot; not very attractive with a broken road and rusty gate, but there were lots of people, so she thought it was worth checking out. As she gazed into the water from the dilapidated looking parking lot, she was astonished to see many yellow and blue fish. She jumped off the side and swam in the warm pristine turquoise water. There were some young girls looking at her from the ledge, so she asked,

"Why are you looking at me?"

"We wonder why you swim with a seal behind you?" a brown-haired girl said.

"A what?" Cherise asked.

"A monk seal is right behind you. Lady, you beddah get outta there now!" A teenage girl yelled.

Cherise turned around and two feet away was this large brown, whiskered seal. She began to swim to the ladder as quickly as she could. One of the girls met her and gave her a hand as she came out.

"It's okay now, you're okay." The brown-haired girl said.

"I didn't know it was there."

"We don't swim here after five o'clock because that's when the seals or sharks come around." The teenage girl said.

"Oh great. I'm glad I'm on land now. Thanks for telling me." Cherise said as she walked over to the shower spigot on the rock.

The experience with the girls reminded her of when she was on Tongue Mountain and the teenagers helped her.

The next morning, she awoke to the sounds of cows, chickens, and birds. Wow, I'm not in New York City, that's for sure, she thought. There was an odd whirling sound too.

"Good morning, Cherise. I'm Hila."

"Oh, hi. I met..."

"Ollie, my wife."

"I didn't realize there were two of you. It's nice to meet you. Your place is incredibly peaceful. I slept better than I have in years."

"That's great to hear. Your coffee is ready and here is your breakfast."

With that, Hila place a beautiful plate of food containing organic scrambled eggs, toast, and local tropical fruit on the table for Cherise.

"What's the whirling sound I heard last night?"

"Oh, that's our windmill." Ollie said as she entered the bamboo building.

"As I mentioned yesterday, we are off grid, meaning the windmill and solar panels produce our electricity which is stored in batteries behind the building where you slept."

"You're not hooked up to power lines?"

"No. So, when the town has a power outage, we have power." Hila said.

They shared breakfast and stories for the next hour. Cherise enjoyed being in the home of a female couple. It felt so comfortable to her. She packed up and said her goodbyes and headed down the road to hike a place called Pololu Valley. As she drove through little Kapa'au Town, she spotted a place called The Courtyard for coffee and decided to stop. She ordered a mocha from the friendly woman, and walked outside where there was a small, attractive grouping of tables on the grass with umbrellas on each one; palm trees and bright red hibiscus flowers surrounding. The temperature was a perfect 80 degrees and there was a light tropical breeze. On her second sip of coffee, she looked up and spit it out across the table because of what she saw. Not what, but who. Cherise stared into those rich brown eyes with no words able to leave her lips.

"Cherise, it's good to see you too." Georgia said with a smile.

"Yeah, yeah, hi. I am shocked to see you. Sit down."

Cherise used a few napkins to wipe up the coffee she splattered across the table as her heart raced with Georgia's very unexpected presence. She felt a wave of excitement mixed with anger and confusion.

"I bet my mother had something to do with this." Georgia said calmly.

"You mean your mother who came through at the séance where you left me stranded like a dog?" Cherise said in a sarcastic tone.

"That would be the one."
Although Georgia was surprised at this chance meeting, she felt an unusual sense of calm.

"Is it possible, now that your mother and the universe has brought us to meet here in Kohala, you could share what the heck happened that night?"

"As a matter of fact, I could, right after I have my coffee." Georgia said.

With that, Cherise, dramatically let out a big sigh and flung her arm on the table followed by her head.

"What are the chances we'd meet up here like this?" Georgia asked to Cherise as the restaurant owner delivered her coffee and slice of scrumptious looking banana bread.

"Excuse me, but can I ask if you've grown up here?" Cherise asked the petite woman.

"Not in this area, but in Honolulu."

"It feels very different here than on Oahu." Georgia said.

"Hawaii is a pretty magical place, but Kohala is quite special, in my opinion." She replied.

"Coincidentally, the two of us met up here, not knowing the other was traveling to Hawaii, all the way from New York." Cherise said with confusion.

"Have you two heard of Pele, the goddess of fire, who resides on this island in the volcano?"
They shook their heads back and forth as they stared at the woman, with a look of expectation and excitement in their eyes.

"You might like to pick up a book about her and the strong energy that inhabits this place to better understand the synchronicity happening with you. Anyway, enjoy your coffee and your time here in Kohala. I need to get back to work. Aloha ladies."
Off she went as the two women sat quietly, taking in the information they just received. Then Georgia took a sip of her coffee, cleared her throat, and began to share her story.

"It was about ten years when I met Kwesi on a tennis court. We had an instant attraction and within months, I found myself pregnant. He was clear that he did not want to get married but would be there for our child and me. I was happy about having a child but was not sure that the timing was very good. It was something I wanted in my future, but not right then. Clearly, the universe had another idea. I'd considered abortion, but didn't feel I could live with myself, so I made the decision to keep the baby. The pregnancy was uneventful, until the last month. The doctor said the baby was breech, feet first and my blood pressure was very high, so she confined me to bed rest. I went into labor a few weeks early, and Kwesi was away in Ghana with his ailing father, so I was alone. It lasted 30 hours and my blood pressure was so high, they were concerned

I'd go into cardiac arrest, but just as they told me they'd be doing a cesarean, I dilated and within minutes, my son was born."

Cherise is listening intently as Georgia begins to tear up. She takes a napkin to wipe her eyes, has a sip of coffee and continues.

"The moment of his birth, I experienced a joy unlike anything I'd known before. When they placed him on me and I gazed into his velvety black eyes, I felt an instant connection. It sounds cliché, but it was very deep. I knew my life had changed and I would be a better person knowing this new little being. Kwesi offered to cut his trip short, but I said I'd be fine. We arrived home by taxi two days later and three weeks later, after a long day of his crying, I put Randy in his crib to sleep. When I awoke five hours later, I felt something must be wrong because he hadn't woken me up as he'd been doing, every two to three hours. As I looked in on him, I saw he wasn't moving. I picked him up and his little body was lifeless and cool."

Georgia is crying but puts her hand up to Cherise who wants to interrupt.

"Let me finish, please. I called 911 and slumped to the floor. My heart hurt so much; I couldn't think. I sat holding him, crying until they arrived. When they took him from me, I called my mother and she met me at the hospital. Of course, there was nothing they could do to revive him, and it was considered a SIDS death. Three months later, without warning, my mother died in her sleep. Her death put me in a state of shock. My mind told me she left to be with him and watch over him, but I was heartbroken. There was no consoling me. Over time, I became functional, but it's only now that I can tell you this without feeling like I will die."

Cherise got up and sat next to Georgia and looked into her wet, teary eyes as she said

"Georgia, thank you for sharing. I am so sorry for all the loss and heart ache and now have a better understanding why you ran out that night. "

"I wasn't ready to hear that message from my mother. It was overwhelming as it opened the floodgates of emotions, I hadn't been able to feel for so long. I came to Hawai'i to take time for me; to heal and relax."

"Can I share a recent message from séance?" Cherise asked.

"Yes, please."

"It was your mother apologizing for upsetting you and saying she wants only for your happiness. She said that Randy sits on the red-checkered window seat in your living room each night and that he does not blame you, he loves you."

"I am happy. I'm happy to have met you and am ready for a new adventure. How about you?" Georgia said.

"I was bitten by a snake and am smitten with you, Georgia Clay. Yes, I'm ready." Cherise said.

About the Author

Eila's passion for writing began as a child, writing letters to her aunts. She has published "Estuary", An Interdimensional Poetic Journey, "On the Road to Bliss" A Poetic Journey, "Rhapsody in Bohemia" plus numerous pieces in newspapers, magazines, and anthologies.

Her certification in Transformative Language Arts inspires her to bring spoken word events to the community. The pandemic restrictions motivated her to create via ZOOM, a recorded YouTube show "Inside the Writers Studio" presented by the Hawaii Writers Guild, featuring a different writer each program.

Her passion is to give voice to the invisible, whether emotions, actions, or experiences with the unseen world of Spirit and she's committed to writing and speaking her truth.

As a radio personality she shares her love of music and spoken work on Womens Voices on one program. Another show, Intuitive Talk Story, is a talk show where she and her co-host channel wisdom and knowledge from their higher selves and Spirit.

Books by Eila Algood

Estuary

Rhapsody in Bohemia

On the Road to Bliss